This Starfish Bay book belongs to

• • • • • • • • • • • • • • • • • • • • • • • • • • • • • • • • • • • • • • • • • • • • • • • • • • • • • • • • • • • • • • •

# The Wooden Fish

Starfish Bay® Children's Books
An imprint of Starfish Bay Publishing
www.starfishbaypublishing.com

THE WOODEN FISH

ISBN 978-1-76036-064-1
First Published 2019
Printed in China by Toppan Leefung Printing Limited
20th Floor, 169 Electric Road, North Point, Hong Kong

Text Copyright © 2010 by Wenxuan CAO
Illustrations Copyright © 2010 by Yanling GONG
Originally published as "一条大鱼向东游" in Chinese
English translation rights from Tomorrow Publishing House
All rights reserved

Thank you to Courtney Chow, Marlo Garnsworthy and Na Zhou (in alphabetical order) who were involved in translating and editing this book.

Our thanks also go out to Elyse Williams for her creative efforts in preparing this edition for publication.

37123001024410

# The Wooden Fish

Written by Wenxuan CAO
Illustrated by Yanling GONG

There was a great river flowing all year round.

There were no bridges, but a few boats floated upon it.

The villagers had planned to build a bridge over the river, but for some strange reason, only one wooden post was ever put up.
That wooden post stood amid the river, lonely.

The wooden post had thought that, one by one, more wooden
posts would appear. Together they would hold up a big bridge.
Instead, it waited day after day, but no one came by.
So, it had no choice but to wait.

One night, it had a brilliant dream. It dreamed the river was full of tall wooden posts. Children jumped from one wooden post to another. The water swirled between the posts as the children laughed happily.

Sadly, it woke up to find the river was as empty as before.
It was still the only wooden post in the river.
It was clear that there wasn't going to be a bridge.

Even in the skies, a star was not alone.
One star would always be surrounded by other twinkling stars.

The flying wild goose in the sky, too, was not alone. The wild geese flew together in one long formation, as if someone had drawn a line in the sky.
Nor was the white poplar alone on earth. They stood one after another, extending out toward the distant horizon.

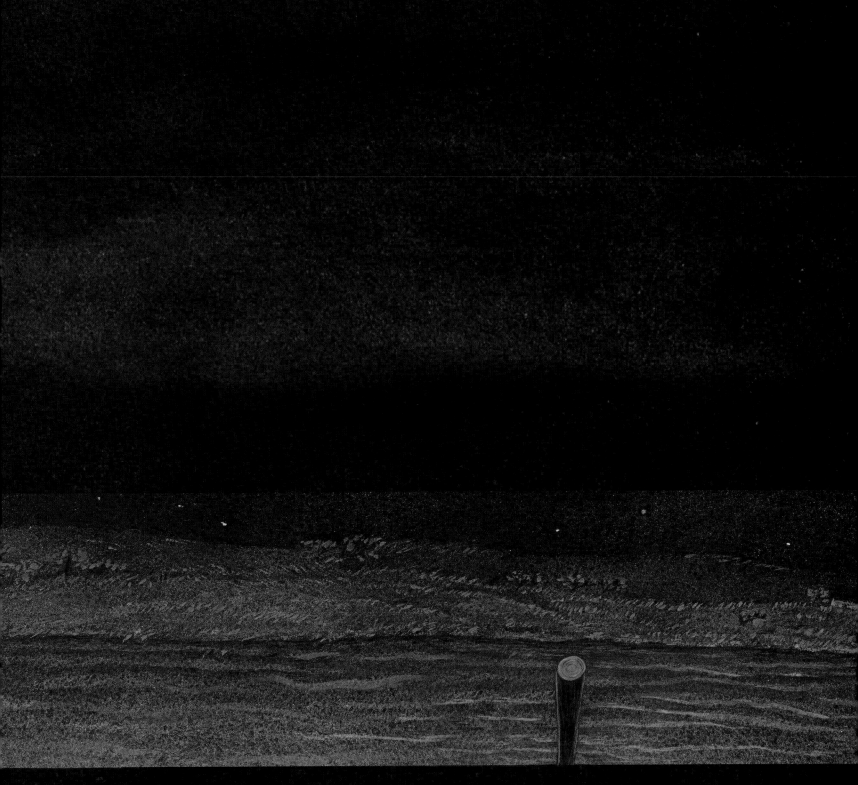

In the middle of the great river, however, the wooden post was alone.

When spring came, small leaves grew on the post.
An egret landed on it.
The egret used the wooden post to sharpen its claws and beak. The wooden post felt pain, yet it was full of happiness.
Even when the egret left its droppings on the post and dirtied it, the wooden post wanted to reassure the egret, "It doesn't matter. I'll be good as new after it rains."
The wooden post didn't want the egret to leave.

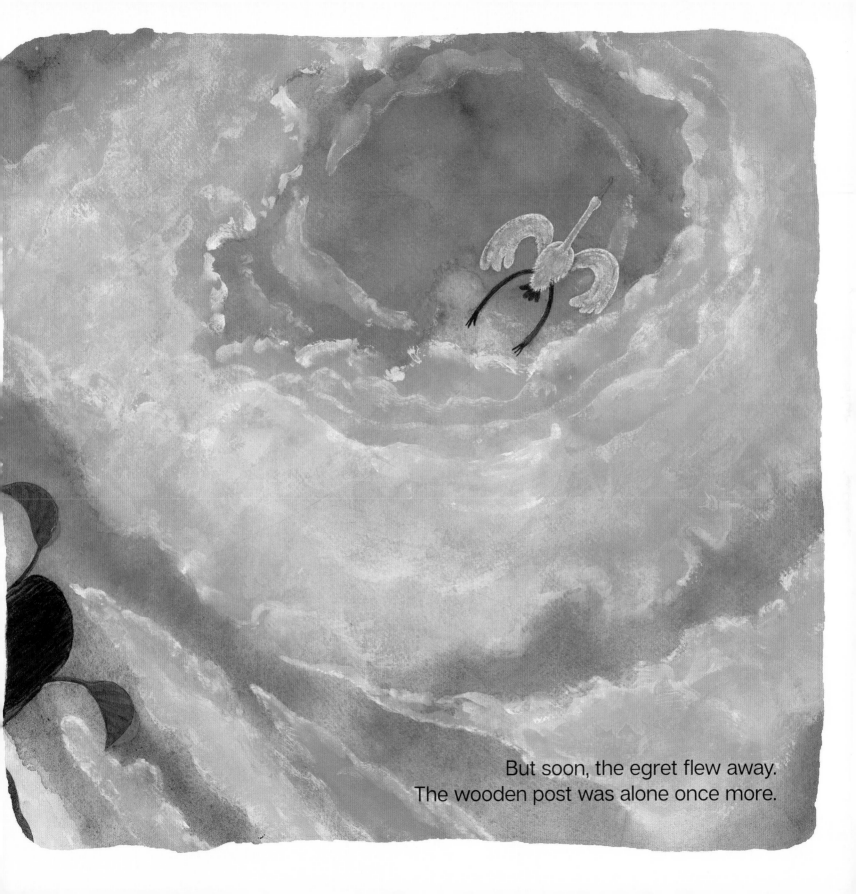

But soon, the egret flew away.
The wooden post was alone once more.

One evening, an old fisherman tied his boat to the wooden post. It looked like the fisherman would be staying the night! The wooden post was full of joy, its leaves swaying in the wind.

The fisherman sat at the end of his boat, looking up at the stars in the sky, singing...
His song was a sad one.
The wooden post listened intently.
Even its leaves were still and quiet.
The fisherman sang until the moon sank into the distant reeds.

Once the moonlight had faded, the
fisherman went to sleep.
A hush descended on the great river.
The wooden post thought, "What a
beautiful night it is."

One day, a shepherd boy sat on the riverbank, while his sheep fed on the grass. He cupped his chin silently, sitting still.

After a while, the boy began to throw mud, clay, and stones at the post. Again and again he tried, but he missed each time.
The wooden post wanted to move so the boy would be able to hit it. But it had no choice but to remain motionless, stuck in one spot.

That shepherd boy came every day,
never speaking or singing.
He always sat quietly, aiming for the
wooden post with mud, clay, and stones.
Then...
Ha! He finally hit the post!
The wooden post felt pain, but above all, it felt joy.
The leaves rustled as if they were clapping.

Soon, the shepherd boy's aim became perfect. He hit his target each time he threw.
Despite being scratched, the wooden post was happy. It was happy that the shepherd boy kept him company every day. It was happy, even if the shepherd boy threw things at him, each throw fiercer than the last.

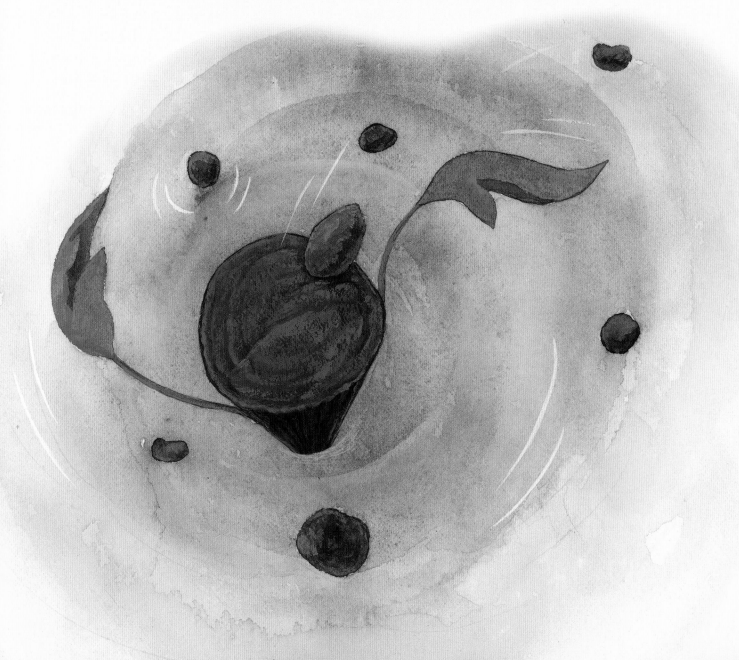

When autumn came, it was stormy every day.
Everything was shrouded in a light, misty veil.
To the wooden post's disappointment, the shepherd boy
no longer appeared on the riverbank.

One day, the flood came, ruining some villages.
A child was being carried away by the strong current!

The shepherd boy's frightened eyes caught sight of the familiar wooden post.
It was the shepherd boy in the water!
The wooden post shouted with no sound, "Grab on to me! You must!"
The moment the shepherd boy was close enough, he flung his arms around it.
The water came crashing against the wooden post with increasing force. The wooden post began to tilt.
A huge wave smashed against the wooden post, uprooting it. It began to float down the river.
The shepherd boy tightened his hold, braving the waves.
The wooden post was moving! It was an extraordinary moment.

Fortunately, a wave carried the shepherd boy back to the shore.
The strong waves caused the wooden post to spin and spin.
Soon, it was amid everything else that had been carried away by the flood.

The shepherd boy coughed and spluttered,
watching the wooden post from the shore.
Gradually, he could no longer tell which piece was
the wooden post that had saved him.
To the shepherd boy, they looked like fish set free,
swimming far, far away.

# The Author

Wenxuan Cao was born in 1954 in Yancheng, Jiangsu, China, and is a professor of Chinese literature at Peking University. As one of China's most esteemed children's books writers, he has published dozens of works and won more than 40 awards. His work has been translated into English, French, German, Japanese, Korean, and more. In 2016, he became the first Chinese author to receive the Hans Christian Andersen Award. His works express his concern for the lifestyle and emotional well-being of children and adolescents.

# The Illustrator

Yanling Gong was born in 1973 in Nanjing, China. Since she created her first children's picture book in 2004, she has illustrated many other children's picture books. Her work was shortlisted at the 2015 Biennial of Illustrations Bratislava. She enjoys reading, drawing, and cleansing her heart with fairy tales.